F.R.

• 4056V

D1509733

This book belongs to:

South Hanover Elementary School

Morgan the Dog™

To all the dogs, cats, and other creatures
who are waiting to meet their "Brittany."

To order "Morgan the Dog" books and products, call 1-800-247-6553.

MORGAN THE DOG and MORGAN design are trademarks of
Morgan House Publishing

Submit permission requests to:
Morgan House Publishing
President/Editor: Janet Synnestvedt Friesen
www.morganthedog.com

Written by: Heather Irbinskas
Original story: Susan Carlberg
Illustrations: Andra King
Editor/Consultant: Maureen Sullivan
Publishing consultant: Five Star Publications, Inc.
Book design: Alison Josephs

Printed in the U.S.A.
Library of Congress
ISBN: 0-9711970-0-8

Introducing "Morgan the Dog"

The Morgan the Dog series was inspired by a young single mother with the support of her family and friends. Shanda Friesen wanted her daughter, Brittany, to have access to quality Internet programs that enhance learning while imparting valuable life lessons.

Shanda and Brittany were also enthralled with their dog, Morgan, whose antics and unique personality were legendary in the family. So we created a series of books and a related web site for children that would entertain and help them learn through Morgan's adventures. Based on real life and imaginary stories, "Morgan the Dog" entered into the world of books and the Internet, as family members and friends rallied behind Shanda's idea, each taking on a task to help her dream come true.

This first book and companion web site mark the beginning of a series of Morgan adventures. The stories capture Morgan's personality and the special relationship between a young child and her dog.

Morgan is a mixed-breed dog, who in the beginning doubts himself, then learns he is regal in every sense. In that regard, he represents the uniqueness and fallibility in all of us. Yet, he rises above his humble background to accomplish extraordinary things with the help and love of Brittany and her friends.

We hope you join us on all of Morgan's adventures. If your child enjoys the ride and learns along the way, Shanda's vision for Brittany will truly have been met.

Bob Marshall
Publisher

My name is Morgan, and I believe in magic.
I believe in happy days and cozy nights, rides in cars and friends for life!
I didn't always, though. You see, I used to live in an animal shelter.

My life changed the day a little girl named Brittany
came to the shelter looking for a dog.

I saw her walk slowly down the row of cages,
looking at every dog.

"Pick me!"
barked the terrier.

"Take me,"
woofed the Lab.

I lay curled under my blanket. No one seemed to want me, the little corgi. Well, not exactly a corgi! Most corgis have short legs and no tail. I am of mixed-breed heritage, so my legs are long and I have a fluffy white tail! Since I came to the shelter, most of the other dogs that were here are now gone. Adopted. So who would want me?

"Look, Mom, that blanket just moved!"
"Who's there?" Brittany asked as she peered into my cage.

"Me?" I wondered.
"Could she be talking to me?"
I crawled out from beneath the blanket.
I lifted my nose to her face.

Brittany smiled. "He's so cute!
Does he have a name? What kind of dog is he?"

"His name is Morgan, and he is a Welsh corgi mix," said Andy, the adoption worker.
"Did you know that the corgi is the Queen of England's favorite dog?"
Then he smiled and said, "Even though Morgan is a mix, he could still be your favorite dog.
Every dog here deserves a loving home."

Brittany looked right into my eyes and said,
"I know he's mixed. He's mixed with magic!"

Brittany and I went to the shelter's play yard to make sure that I was the dog she really wanted. I was so excited. I hoped she would like me. We played, we laughed, and we tumbled.

In the yard there was also a black Labrador named Cody with a boy named Brian. We made new friends. We all played together. We were having so much fun that we didn't notice that the sky had blackened. A big storm was coming!

All of a sudden, the air crackled with lightning.
KABOOM!! crashed the thunder. **WHOOSH!!** howled the wind and rain.
I yelped. I panicked. I ran through an opening in the gate and out of the play yard.

"Morgan! Come back!" yelled Brittany. But I was too scared.
Down the grassy hill I ran, the sound of my heart pounding in my ears.
KABOOM!! the sound was even louder than before!

"It's only thunder. Please, come back!" Brittany cried,
rain and tears streaming down her face.

Brittany's mom and others from the shelter yard tried to follow us, but it all happened so fast. We were too far ahead.

The grassy hill became a slippery slope,
and the little girl lost her balance.

I heard her cries and turned to see
Brittany fall into the creek.

"Help! Help me!" she screamed. I looked around.
The others were still too far away.

I had to do something.

I jumped in and swam. I raced to my friend. The cold, dark water swirled around us.
I grabbed her dress with my teeth and pulled. I wanted to get my Brittany safe again. I was too small
and not strong enough, so I crawled back onto the bank.

I barked and I howled. The water was taking my friend away.
Worse still, it was flowing toward the mouth of a large storm drain.

My friend was in trouble. I saw a branch along the bank and grabbed it with my teeth.

I raced ahead and jumped back into the water.

Struggling, I swam toward the storm drain and blocked its entrance with the branch.

Brittany saw me and grabbed onto the branch.
We held on tight until help arrived.

Soon strong hands pulled us from the rushing water, and loving arms hugged us tight.

"Morgan is magic!" Brittany said, "He saved me, Mom! Did you see?"

"Yes, and I'm so happy you are safe," said Brittany's mom with teary eyes,
"Morgan is special! Let's take you and our new dog home!"

I wagged my tail as Brittany hugged me. I found a home at last.

Brittany's mother pulled a box out of her purse.

Inside was a red collar with a special locket.
"This collar belonged to my dog, when I was your age," she said,
"I thought you might like it for your new best friend."

It fit perfectly.

My name is Morgan, and now you know *why* I believe in magic.

Morgan the Dog™

LOOKING FOR A PET?

If you're looking for a dog or cat for your family, Morgan hopes you'll consider going to your local animal shelter. Some of these animals have had a pretty rough life and they're all looking for a home with people who will love them and take good care of them. Who knows? You might just find the perfect pet for you!

When it comes to dogs, animal shelters usually have purebred dogs as well as mixed-breed dogs like Morgan. Whichever one you choose, make sure it's the right one for your family and for your house and yard. You might think that purebred dogs are the best. But remember, some of the smartest and bravest dogs in the world are mixed-breed dogs. Just ask Morgan!

To learn more about adopting a pet, go to **www.morganthedog.com**.

Questions for Parents and Teachers to Use in Discussing Morgan the Dog with Young Readers

In this story, there are really two rescues that take place. Can you name them?

Why do you think Brittany went to an animal shelter instead of a pet store to look for a dog?

Why did Brittany find Morgan to be special, even though he is a mixed-breed dog?

Morgan is of mixed-breed heritage. What does "heritage" mean?

What steps should you take in a thunderstorm to avoid danger?

Why do you think Brittany's mother wanted her to have the collar and locket?

To learn more about these questions, plus fun games and activities, visit **morganthedog.com**

While you are there, you can join Morgan's online fan club for free!